For you

With love

Something to Remember Me By

by Susan V. Bosak
with illustrations by Laurie McGaw

St. Louis de Montfort Catholic School
Fishers, IN

SCHOLASTIC INC.
New York Toronto London Auckland Sydney
Mexico City New Delhi Hong Kong

ISBN 0-439-12954-0

12 11 10 9 8 7 6 5 4 3 2 1   9/9 0 1 2 3 4/0

Printed in the Mexico   49

First Scholastic printing, September 1999

This is a true story
based on the author's relationship with
and dedicated to
her very dear grandmother, Eva Krawchuk.

It is also a universal story
that echoes the close bond
between the illustrator's daughter and
her grandmother, Kathleen Phillips.

They have given us much to remember them by.

THEY WERE SPECIAL TIMES.

Every time the little girl visited her grandmother, the house smelled so good – homemade soup and roast chicken and fresh-baked cookies.

The house was happy on sunny days and cozy on rainy days. It was always fun.

The little girl could have a snack anytime she wanted.

She could use the big box of crayons in the kitchen drawer to add drawings to the pad of clean, white paper that was just for her.

She could chatter about everything and ask questions by the dozen.

And if she spilled her juice, her grandmother would just wipe it up, saying that accidents happen to little people and big people. Then her grandmother would smile a big, warm smile and give the little girl a warm, snuggly hug.

T HE LITTLE GIRL
visited her
grandmother often.
  Her grandmother
always had time to go
for a walk or play a
game of cards.

Sometimes grandmother
and granddaughter would
go grocery shopping
together. The little girl
could choose whatever she
wanted her grandmother
to cook for dinner.

Sometimes grandmother and granddaughter would get ready for a party for friends and relatives. The little girl would figure out exactly the right place to put each shiny spoon and knife and fork.

Sometimes grandmother and granddaughter would water the garden at the back of the house, or pick beans or pull carrots.

AND SOMETIMES grandmother and granddaughter would just sit and watch television together.

The grandmother would get an apple and a paring knife from the kitchen. Only big people could use the knife, she would tell her granddaughter.

Then the grandmother would carefully peel the apple, letting the strands of red fall to the napkin in her lap. She would cut the apple in half, dig out the core, and slice big wedges of the juicy fruit for the both of them to munch on.

"You're the best grandmother in the whole world!"
the little girl would say.

The grandmother would smile a big, warm smile and
give her granddaughter a warm, snuggly hug.

AT THE END of one of the visits, the grandmother took her granddaughter's hand and led her into the bedroom.

"I want to give you something to remember me by," the grandmother started. "Someday, that cedar chest at the foot of the bed will be yours. But for now, I want you to have this."

She handed her granddaughter a wooden doll. It wore a pale yellow dress with white flowers on it. The painted face had bright red lips and big, wide-open eyes with long eyelashes.

Aفter that, many of the visits ended in the same way. Grandmother and granddaughter would go into the bedroom and the grandmother would say exactly the same thing:

"I want to give you something to remember me by. Someday, that cedar chest at the foot of the bed will be yours. But for now, I want you to have this."

And then the grandmother would give her granddaughter this or that.

As the girl grew, so did the number of things her grandmother gave her – a stuffed bear with soft, white fur; a carved wooden flute; a china figurine of a boy and a small puppy; a shiny, copper-colored coin with strange writing on it; a fancy pen that you had to use with special ink; a round, gold watch on a thick chain; a silver picture frame; and a flowery, orange and red and brown and blue tablecloth (that tablecloth was the one thing the girl thought was *really ugly*, but she took it and said "thank you" as always).

Once, the girl asked why her grandmother gave her all these things to remember her by.

The grandmother smiled a big, warm smile and gave her granddaughter a warm, snuggly hug.

"Because everyone wants to be remembered," said the grandmother simply.

The girl didn't quite understand.

THE GIRL grew up into a young woman. She moved far away.

But she and her grandmother would talk on the phone often. This was very exciting for the grandmother. It was a long distance call and she didn't get many of those.

The grandmother would listen all about the young woman's work and about her new family. She was so proud of her granddaughter.

At the end of one telephone call, the grandmother told her granddaughter to watch for a package in the mail.

The next week, a small box filled with tissue paper arrived. Nestled deep in the tissue was a handsewn cushion in the shape of a heart. It was stitched with big purple flowers, tiny pink flowers, and special lettering.

There was a note with the cushion: "Something to remember me by."

T HERE CAME A DAY when the grandmother made an important long distance call to her granddaughter. It was time to come and get the cedar chest. The grandmother was moving out of her house.

The grandmother couldn't take care of the house any more. She couldn't see as well as she used to. She couldn't hear as well as she used to. Her hands didn't work as well as they used to. And she was getting forgetful. She couldn't remember some times and places and names.

So, the young woman came to get the cedar chest and to help her grandmother pack.

WHEN ALL THE PACKING was done, grandmother and granddaughter stood and looked at the empty house.

The granddaughter was sad. The house was a very special place for her.

The grandmother was sad too – but not about the house. It was time to leave the house. Something else was bothering her.

"I'm worried," said the grandmother. "I'm forgetting too many things."

"Everyone forgets things," responded her granddaughter reassuringly.

"But," said the grandmother softly, "I'm scared that... that I'm going to forget *you*."

The young woman was silent.

She looked at her grandmother. She thought for a moment.

THE YOUNG WOMAN reached over to the important boxes that her grandmother had insisted go with them in the car. She ripped the tape off the top of one box and rummaged through it.

Finally, she found the photograph she was looking for – of grandmother and granddaughter.

In big, bold letters, the granddaughter wrote both their names on the back of the photograph.

"Something to remember me by," said the young woman as she handed the photograph to her grandmother.

The grandmother smiled a big, warm smile and gave her granddaughter a warm, snuggly hug.

TIME PASSED.

The grandmother wasn't well, and was very, very old. The granddaughter traveled once again to see her.

When the young woman walked into her grandmother's room, she expected a big, warm smile and a warm, snuggly hug, like always.

But there was only a blank look.

The young woman put down the flowers she had brought. "It's me. It's your granddaughter. It's me." she repeated, not believing her grandmother wouldn't remember her.

But the grandmother only looked confused.

The young woman sat down by the bed. She talked to her grandmother while she was awake. She held her grandmother's hand when she fell asleep.

For the BEST
Grandmother,
With Love

THE GRANDMOTHER'S HAND was small and wrinkled, but it was soft and warm. The granddaughter stroked the hand and she whispered, "You're the best grandmother in the whole world."

The grandmother opened her eyes. And then, for a moment, she smiled that big, warm smile!

The grandmother turned her head toward the drawer beside the bed.

The young woman opened the drawer. Inside was the old photograph of grandmother and granddaughter.

The edges were tattered and one corner of the photograph was bent. The writing on the back was smudged…

THE YOUNG WOMAN went back to her home, her work, and her family.

The cedar chest sat in her bedroom, at the foot of the bed. The chest was filled with all the special things the grandmother had given her granddaughter.

The young woman knelt beside the chest and opened it slowly. She looked through the contents. She could almost hear her grandmother's words, "I want to give you something to remember me by."

But the young woman's heart really didn't need any of the things to remember her grandmother.

Her grandmother had given her much more than would ever fit in the cedar chest.

As the young woman looked up from the cedar chest, she noticed her reflection in the dresser mirror. She got up and went to the mirror.

She looked closely. She looked for a long time.

And then she smiled a big, warm smile – her grandmother's smile.

About the Author

Something to Remember Me By is based on Susan Bosak's fond memories of her relationship with her "Baba", which is "Grandmother" in Ukrainian. She still has all of the things her grandmother gave her, including the cedar chest, which sits proudly at the foot of her bed.

With a master's degree in the social science of human communication, Susan Bosak is a researcher, educator, and word weaver. She has a special interest in the power of stories as a form of communication. She has written several books, including the bestselling activity book *Science Is…*, which takes an innovative approach to communicating with children about science. She lives and works with her husband and brother on a tranquil country property near Toronto, Canada.

About the Illustrator

Laurie McGaw created the characters in *Something to Remember Me By* using a real family as models – grandmother Maureen Viegener, her granddaughters Melissa Tratt, 7, and Sarah Tratt, 11, and her daughter Mary Anne Tratt (who posed for the grown granddaughter). Warm thanks go to each of them.

Whether in editorial illustrations, advertising work, or commissioned portraits, Laurie McGaw's special talent is portraying people. She particularly enjoys children's book illustration and has done several books, including *The Secrets of Vesuvius*, the award-winning *Polar The Titanic Bear*, *The Illustrated Father Goose*, and *Discovering The Iceman*. She lives in the Mulmur Hills near Toronto, Canada with her husband and two young children.

This book is one of the creative works of The Communication Project. Founded in 1984, we are a research and education group involved in exploring many areas of human communication. For more information on our books, story sessions, and communication workshops, or to be included on our mailing list, write to The Communication Project, 9 Lobraico Lane, Whitchurch-Stouffville, Ontario, L4A 7X5, Canada; or call us at (905) 640-8914 or 1-800-772-7765.